LOST IN THE MOUSEUM

by **Eleanor May** • Illustrated by **Deborah Melmon**

THE KANE PRESS / NEW YORK

To Mrs. Bryant's kindergarten class—E.M.
For Jeanne, my museum advisor and friend—D.M.

Acknowledgments: We wish to thank the following people for their helpful advice and review of the material contained in this book: Susan Longo, Early Childhood and Elementary School Teacher, Mamaroneck, NY; and Rebeka Eston Salemi, Kindergarten Teacher, Lincoln School, Lincoln, MA.

Special thanks to Susan Longo for providing the Fun Activities in the back of this book.

Library of Congress Cataloging-in-Publication Data

May, Eleanor.
Lost in the Mouseum / by Eleanor May ; illustrated by Deborah Melmon.
pages cm. — (Mouse math)
"With fun activities!"
Summary: Mouse friends Albert and Leo search left and right for Penny when she goes missing at the Mouseum.
ISBN 978-1-57565-643-4 (library reinforced binding : alk. paper) — ISBN 978-1-57565-644-1 (pbk. : alk. paper)
[1. Left and right—Fiction. 2. Mice—Fiction. 3. Museums—Fiction. 4. Missing children—Fiction.]
I. Melmon, Deborah, illustrator. II. Title.
PZ7.M4513Lo 2015
[E]—dc23
2014038449

eISBN: 978-1-57565-645-8

1 3 5 7 9 10 8 6 4 2

First published in the United States of America in 2015 by Kane Press, Inc.
Printed in the United States of America

Book Design: Edward Miller

Mouse Math is a registered trademark of Kane Press, Inc.

Visit us online at **www.kanepress.com**

 Like us on Facebook
facebook.com/kanepress

Follow us on Twitter
@KanePress

Dear Parent/Educator,

"I can't do math." Every child (or grownup!) who says these words has at some point along the way felt intimidated by math. For young children who are just being introduced to the subject, we wanted to create a world in which math was not simply numbers on a page, but a part of life—an adventure!

Enter Albert and Wanda, two little mice who live in the walls of a People House. Children will be swept along with this irrepressible duo and their merry band of friends as they tackle mouse-sized problems and dilemmas (and sometimes *cat-sized* problems and dilemmas!).

Each book in the **MOUSE MATH**® series provides a fresh take on a basic math concept. The mice discover solutions as they, for instance, use position words while teaching a pet snail to do tricks or count the alarmingly large number of friends they've invited over on a rainy day—and, lo and behold, they are doing math!

Math educators who specialize in early childhood learning have applied their expertise to make sure each title is as helpful as possible to young children—and to their parents and teachers. Fun activities at the ends of the books and on our website encourage kids to think and talk about math in ways that will make each concept clear and memorable.

As with our award-winning Math Matters® series, our aim is to captivate children's imaginations by drawing them into the story, and so into the math at the heart of each adventure. It is our hope that kids will want to hear and read the **MOUSE MATH** stories again and again and that, as they grow up, they will approach math with enthusiasm and see it as an invaluable tool for navigating the world they live in.

Sincerely,

Joanne Kane

Joanne E. Kane
Publisher

Check out these titles in
MOUSE MATH:

Albert Adds Up!
Adding/Taking Away

Albert Is NOT Scared
Direction Words

Albert Keeps Score
Comparing Numbers

Albert's Amazing Snail
Position Words

Albert's BIGGER Than Big Idea
Comparing Sizes: Big/Small

Albert Starts School
Days of the Week

Albert the Muffin-Maker
Ordinal Numbers

A Beach for Albert
Capacity

Count Off, Squeak Scouts!
Number Sequence

Lost in the Mouseum
Left/Right

Mice on Ice
2D Shapes

The Mousier the Merrier!
Counting

A Mousy Mess
Sorting

The Right Place for Albert
One-to-One Correspondence

And visit
www.kanepress.com/
mouse-math
for more!

"What a great day for the Mouseum!" Albert said.
"Which way should we go first?"

His sister, Wanda, pointed **left**. "I'd like to see the mummies."

UNRAVEL THE MYSTERIES OF ANCIENT EGYPT

← LEFT

"Me too!" her friend Lucy said. "Come on, Penny."
She tugged her little cousin's paw.
But Penny wouldn't come.

PAWS-ON

Information

Lucy pulled **left**.

Penny pulled **right**.

"I think she wants to go to the Paws-On Room," Leo said.

LEFT

RIGHT

"I love the Paws-On Room!" Albert said.
"Let's take her there while they go see the mummies."

"Keep an eye on Penny," Lucy warned.

"Don't worry!" Albert said. "We will!"

At the Paws-On Room,
Penny went straight to the sandbox.

Albert and Leo built a bridge . . .

then knocked it down.

After a while, Leo said, "Where's Penny?"

Albert looked around. "Oh, no! She's gone!"

Albert and Leo dashed out to the hall.
No Penny to the **left**.

No Penny to the **right**.

HALL OF PORTRAITS

LEFT

RIGHT

"We've got to find her!" said Leo.
"I'll go **left**. You go **right**."

"Okay!" Albert said.

LEFT

RIGHT

Albert scampered through Mice of the World.
"Penny?" he called.

13

"Yikes!"
Albert stared up at a giant, scary mask.
That *definitely* wasn't Penny.

Albert searched high and low.

But Penny was nowhere to be found.

In the next room, he saw Leo.

"You didn't find Penny either?" Albert asked.

HALL OF SCIENCE

"No, and our sisters will be back soon!" Leo groaned. "Where could she have gone?"

"I came from the **right**, and you came from the **left**." Albert pointed. "The only other way is straight ahead."

LEFT

RIGHT

17

Albert and Leo hurried into the Hall of Science.

"Which way now?" Albert asked.

Leo said, "Let's go **left** for bugs."

"Penny likes bugs?" Albert asked.

"I don't know," Leo said. "But I do!"

The Mouse Times

MICE WALK ON MOON
One small step for Mouse

Astromice say moon is not made of Green Cheese!

LEFT

19

"Hey, wait!" Albert pointed.
"Isn't that Penny going into the giant mouse?"

FOLLOW
THE CHEESE
THROUGH
THE
DIGESTIVE
SYSTEM

20

Albert and Leo raced up the ramp.

Just before the little mouse slid down,
Leo grabbed the back of her dress. "Gotcha!"

It wasn't Penny!

The little mouse wailed. Her mother glared.

"Come on!" Albert grabbed Leo's paw.

They slid **left**. . . .

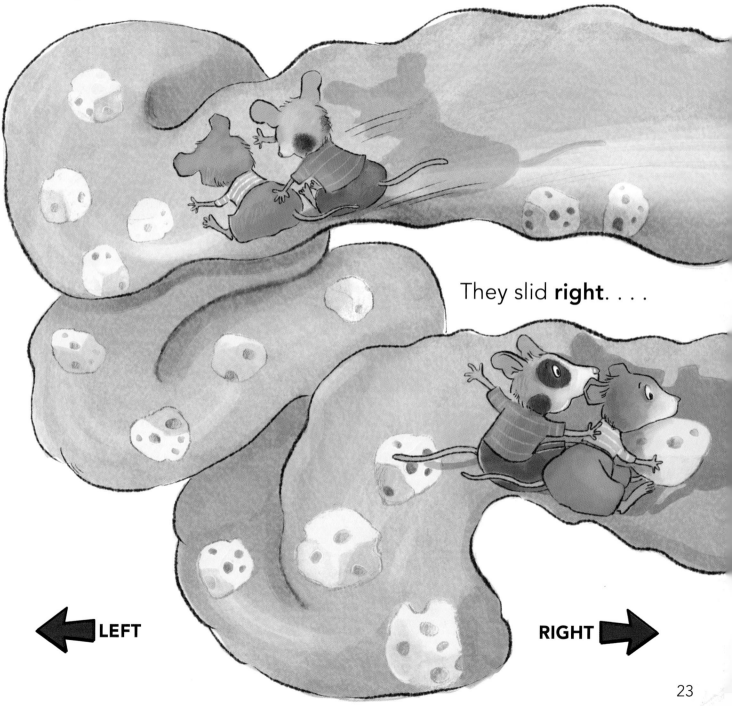

They slid **right**. . . .

◀ LEFT

RIGHT ▶

23

And popped straight out the bottom.

"Let's get out of here!" Leo said.

Albert and Leo scurried toward a doorway.

"We're back at the Paws-On Room!" Albert said.
"And look!"

"PENNY!"

"I don't believe it!" Leo said.
"She was buried in the sand.
She must have been here the whole time!"

Wanda and Lucy came in.

"Thanks for watching Penny!" Lucy said.

"Now it's your turn to see the Mouseum."

Albert looked at Leo.
Leo looked at Albert.

"You know what?" Albert said.
"I think we've seen enough!"

Mummies

Gift Shop

Coat
Check

Restrooms

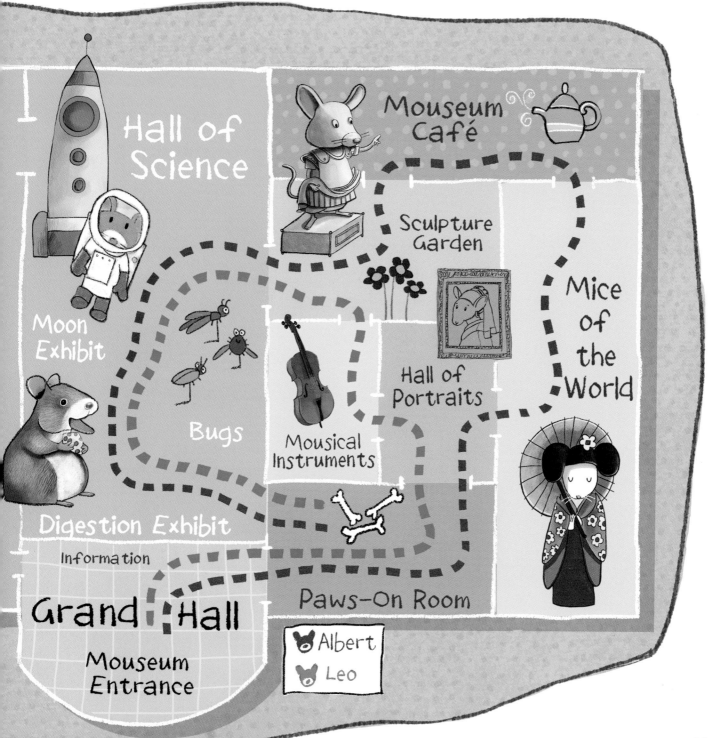

Hall of Science

Mouseum Café

Moon Exhibit

Sculpture Garden

Mice of the World

Bugs

Mousical Instruments

Hall of Portraits

Digestion Exhibit

Information

Grand Hall

Mouseum Entrance

Paws-On Room

Albert
Leo

Lost in the Mouseum supports children's understanding of the **direction words left** and **right**, an important concept in early math learning. Use the activities below to extend the math topic and to support children's early reading skills.

🐭 ENGAGE

Remind children that the cover of a book can tell them a lot about the story inside.

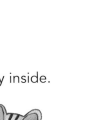

▷ Before reading the title aloud, direct children's attention to the cover illustration. (You may want to conceal the title at first.) Ask: *Where do you think this story takes place?* Ask children if they have ever seen a place that looks like this or if they have seen things like those shown in the illustration. Ask: *What do you think the story might be about?*

▷ Now read the title aloud. Did anyone guess that the story takes place in a museum? Did anyone think that the two mice seem to be lost or that they cannot decide which way to go?

▷ Ask children if they have ever found themselves wondering which way to go, either at home, at school, or in a public building. Encourage children to share their stories and to include details about the place and whom they were with at the time.

▷ Next, ask children how many of them have ever visited a museum. Did they use a floor map of the museum? Why do they think people use maps of museums during their visits?

▷ Now read the story to find out who Albert and Leo think is lost and what they do as they look for that missing mouse!

🐭 LOOK BACK

▶ After reading the story, ask: *Why do Albert and Leo think Penny is lost? Was she really lost? Where is Penny?*

▶ Encourage children to recall the directions in which Albert and Leo turn during their search for Penny. Reread pages 11 and 12, which describe the beginning of Albert and Leo's search for Penny. Emphasize and model the direction words **left** and **right** as you point out that Leo goes left and Albert goes right.

▶ The following activity is optional. Sketch a map similar to the map on pages 28 and 29 on a large sheet of paper or a whiteboard. Use a red marker to show Albert's route and a blue marker to show Leo's route. Point out that the map shows the routes that Albert and Leo took. Write the direction words on the map to identify appropriate turns.

▶ Ask: *What is Penny doing when Albert and Leo finally find her? Is she scared? Why not?*

▶ Ask: *Do Wanda and Lucy know what has really happened?*

▶ Ask: *Why do Albert and Leo say that they don't need to see the rest of the Mouseum at the end of the story?*

🐭 TRY THIS!

Have children help you create a maze with the use of masking tape. Before you begin, review the direction words **left** and **right** on page 6 of the story, as well as the directional arrows on that page. Also point out the direction word **straight** on page 8. Check to be sure that the children understand the meanings of the three direction words. Now create the maze.

▶ Choose a spot to begin the maze and form an "X" on the floor using the masking tape.

▶ Proceed taping the maze throughout the room, turning at right angles both left and right along the way. Say aloud the direction words **left, right,** and **straight** as you go along.

▶ With the masking tape, create a circle on the floor at the end of the maze. (You may want to provide a basket filled with small rewards, such as stickers or pencils, for the children after they successfully navigate the maze.)

▶ Now have the children begin at the "X" and navigate the maze. Encourage them to call out the correct direction words **left, right,** and **straight** as they follow the maze throughout the room.

🐭 THINK!

▶ Have children play a version of the old game "Simon Says." However, this game will be called "Albert Says," and will be played in a slightly different way.

▶ Assign one child to be Albert and stand the child against a wall, facing the room. Have the other children line up in front of "Albert" with their backs to him. (In the game "Simon Says," the children line up several yards away from and facing "Simon." This reversal will allow both "Albert" and the rest of the children to perceive **left** and **right** the same way.)

▶ Then have "Albert" call out directions, such as "Albert says turn right and take two steps," or "Albert says go straight for one step."

▶ If a child does not obey the order correctly, he or she must stand still for the next command. After that, the child can resume the game.

▶ The goal is to reach the opposite wall of the room. When one or more children reach the opposite wall, choose a new "Albert" and play the game again.

◆ FOR MORE ACTIVITIES ◆
visit www.kanepress.com/mouse-math-activities